My Life on the Mountain

HELVETIQ publishing has been supported by the Swiss Federal Office of Culture with a structural grant for the years 2021–2025.

My Life on the Mountain

Originally published as:
Bergère

Text and illustrations: Marion Brand
Design and layout: Marion Brand and Ajša Zdravković
Translation from French: Shona Holmes
Editor: Angela Wade

ISBN: 978-3-03964-056-0
First edition: February 2025
Deposit copy in the Library of Congress: 2025
Printed in China

© 2025 HELVETIQ (Helvetiq SA)
Mittlere Strasse 4
CH-4056 Basel
Switzerland

helvetiq.com

Marion Brand

My Life on the Mountain

Translated by Shona Holmes

4

Good morning!

It's cold this morning.

6

Before going out, I need to light the fire.

Rosie!

Mathilda!

Luna!

It's milking time!

I hope Nanny and Daisy didn't jump over
the fence like they did the other day!

With yesterday's milk, there's enough to make
a new wheel of cheese. Well done, girls!

Behave yourself and wait for me, okay?

Let's go! Quick, quick, to the dairy!

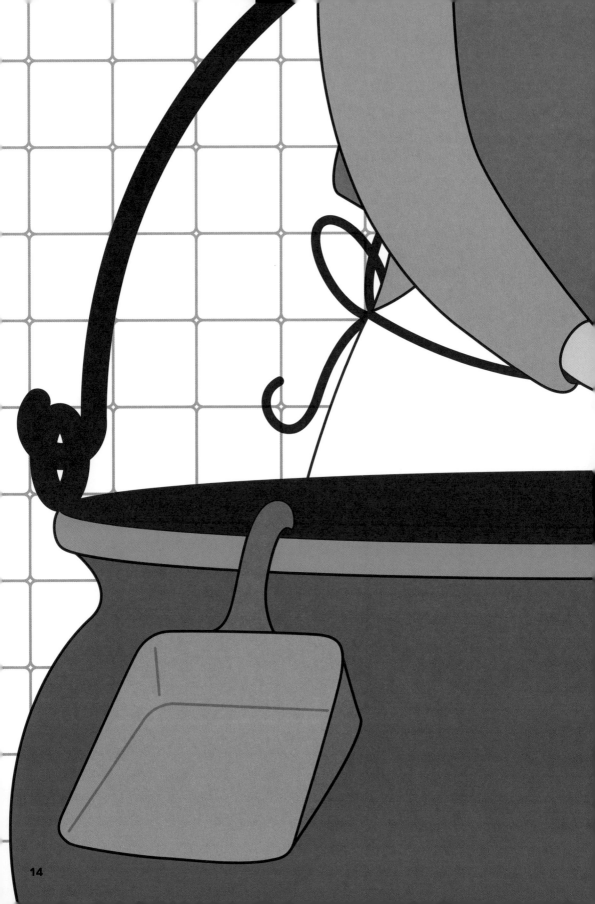

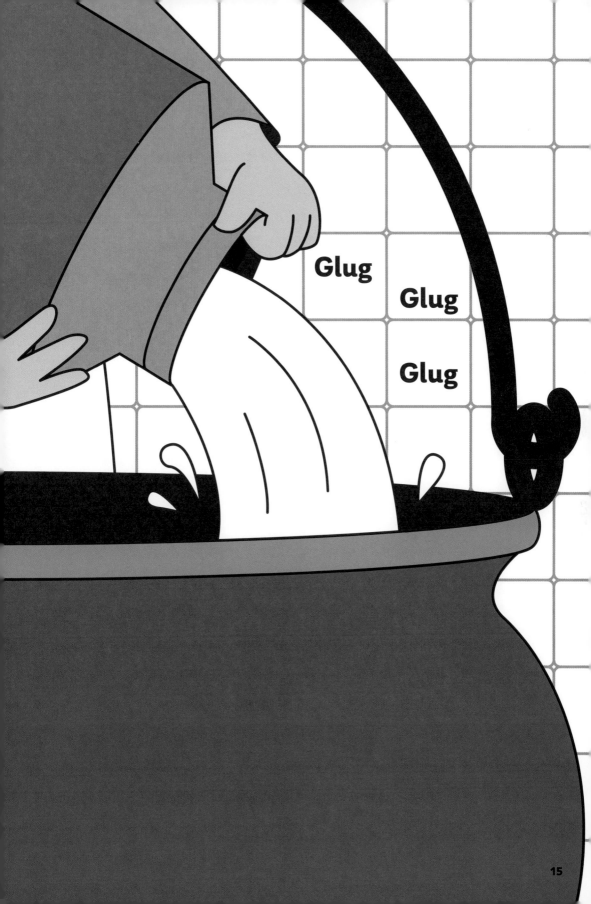

First, cut the curd.

Then return the pot to the heat and stir until the temperature reaches 38°C/100°F.

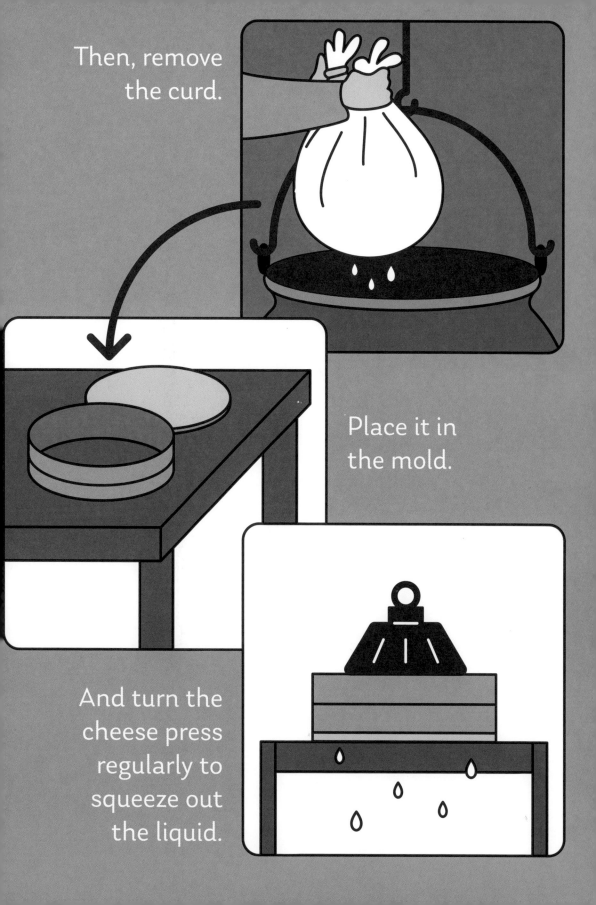

Then, remove the curd.

Place it in the mold.

And turn the cheese press regularly to squeeze out the liquid.

Boing!

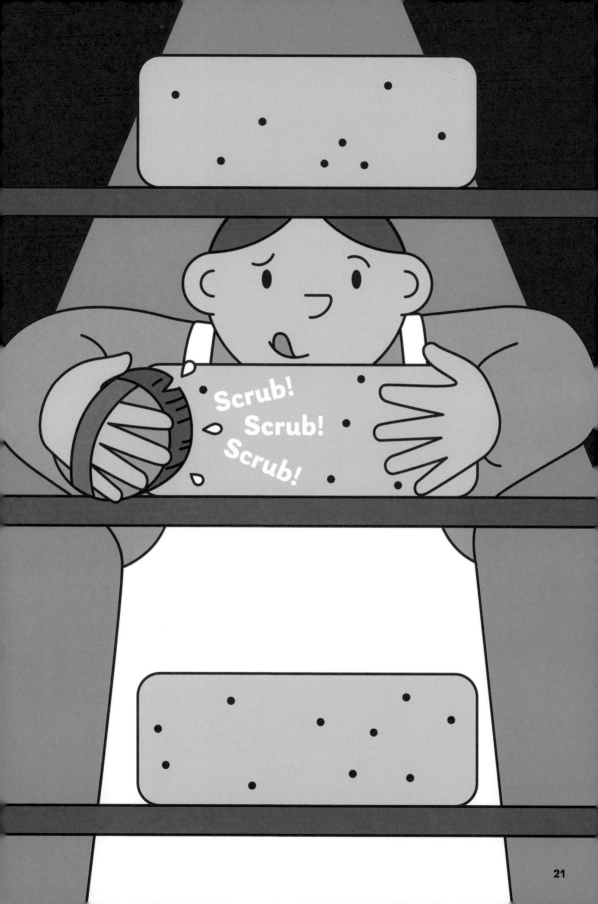

Phew! Time for a break.

All aboard! Off to the village.

Right on time!

Our customers
will be delighted.

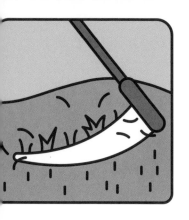

Back home again. Here's some hay
from the valley for the winter...

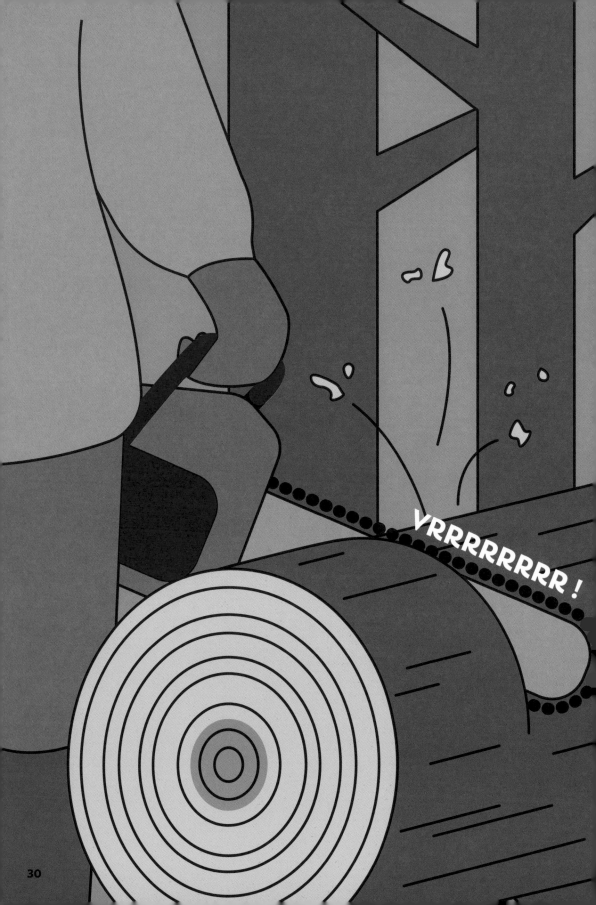

... and some wood for the coming season!

Before the sun goes down...

... here's some grain for you.

And some milk for you!

Another busy day.

There's still a bit of paperwork to be done...

Good night!

Meet a shepherdess!

Can you introduce yourself?

My name is Flavie, I'm Swiss, and I live in the Alps with my dog, Cannelle.

What made you decide to become a herder?

I've always loved nature and animals. When I was little, I spent almost all my free time on the farm with my aunt. When I was a teenager, I had the opportunity to accompany a herd of cows up to the higher pastures where they live in the summer.

I loved life in the mountains: milking the cows early in the morning, tending the fire in the chalet, being close to the wildlife... After that great experience, I took part in the cattle drive to the mountain pastures every year!

What exactly is a cattle drive?

A cattle drive to the mountain pastures is when people move a herd of livestock from a farm to higher grasslands for the summer season. This seasonal move from valleys to pastures is called transhumance. It allows the animals to graze on nutritious grass, which in turn produces good meat and milk.

But not all herders work in the mountains. Elsewhere in the world, farmers and their herds travel hundreds of miles to grassy plains, depending on the weather and the seasons.

What does your job involve?

Herders are responsible for looking after their flock or herd. They check that the animals are in good health and that they have enough to eat. Herders are also responsible for looking after nature, which is their main asset, because taking the animals back to the same place every year to graze means it must be kept healthy.

A herder can also make and sell cheese, prepare wood for the following season, welcome tourists, occasionally go down to the valleys to mow hay... The job has lots of variety.

Is it hard?

Yes, you have to leave your normal home for four to six months and live alone. Most of the work is done outdoors, even when it's cold or raining. The huts are often far from the villages and sometimes there aren't any roads, so you have to walk a long way to do your shopping or see family and friends. Weekends off are out of the question! And even when you're sick or tired, you have to get up early every morning to look after the animals.

But it's also a magical profession where you live peacefully with the rhythm of the seasons and in harmony with nature.

Which animals live on the alp?

Alpine pastures are home to animals that produce milk and provide meat. These are mainly cows, goats and sheep.

But there are also working animals who help people.

Sheepdogs guide the herd and protect it from predators.

Donkeys and horses carry heavy loads.

In the farmyard, pigs drink the whey from the cheesemaking process, and hens lay eggs for the herders' meals.

What do you do with the milk?

By leaving the milk to sit overnight in a large vat, the fat rises to the surface. We use a sieve to remove this extra layer. This is called "skimming."

By beating the cream in a churn, centrifugal force separates the fat from the whey. This is how we get butter.

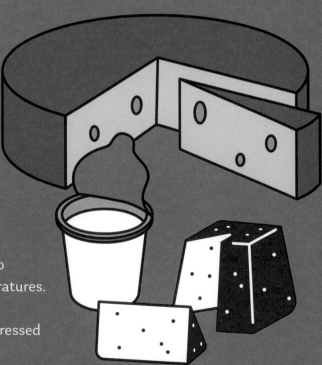

To make yogurts and cheeses, the milk is heated slightly and mixed with bacteria and rennet. This causes it to coagulate into a solid form known as curd.

To make cheese, the curds are cut into pieces and heated to different temperatures.

The curds are then placed in molds, pressed and salted, and left to mature.

Which other animals move with humans?

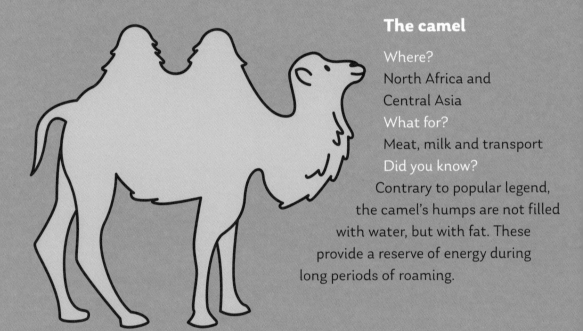

The camel

Where?
North Africa and
Central Asia
What for?
Meat, milk and transport
Did you know?
Contrary to popular legend,
the camel's humps are not filled
with water, but with fat. These
provide a reserve of energy during
long periods of roaming.

The yak

Where?
Himalayan Region
What for?
Meat, milk and wool
Did you know?
The yak, although a bovine like
cows, does not moo but emits a cry
similar to a growl or squeak!

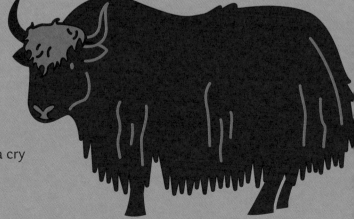

The reindeer

Where?
Most domesticated reindeer are
in northern Europe
What for?
Meat
Did you know?
Reindeer hooves are shaped
like snowshoes to enable them
to walk on snow without sinking.

The zebu

Where?
India, Sub-Saharan Africa
What for?
Meat and milk
Did you know?
The zebu's hump serves as a fat reserve.
This is also the origin of its name, which
comes from the Tibetan word *zeba*,
meaning "hump."

The alpaca

Where?
South America
What for?
Wool and meat
Did you know?
The alpaca lives mainly on the high plateaus
of the Andes. Today, because of global warming,
the herders have more and more difficulty finding
water and grass for their animals.

Where do herders live?

It all depends on the type of transhumance!

When the herd returns to the same place every year, the herders sleep in solid, weatherproof buildings.

Historically, these were wooden chalets, terracotta huts or stone shelters built with local materials by the herders.

When the herd lives entirely outdoors, the herder often lives alone in a small hut without running water or electricity.

Or, sometimes, the buildings can be larger, with additional rooms for milking the animals or making cheese.

When animals and humans are nomadic, these dwellings are more compact, like the caravan, the Mongolian yurt or the Tuareg tent.

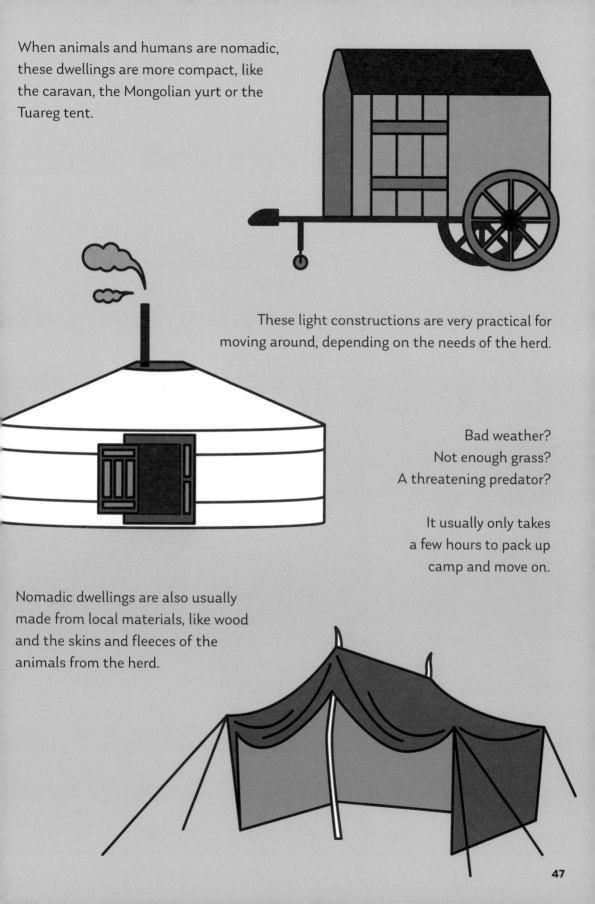

These light constructions are very practical for moving around, depending on the needs of the herd.

Bad weather?
Not enough grass?
A threatening predator?

It usually only takes
a few hours to pack up
camp and move on.

Nomadic dwellings are also usually made from local materials, like wood and the skins and fleeces of the animals from the herd.

Thank you to the people of Arpilles Alp in l'Étivaz
and Col de la Croix Alp in Villars-sur-Ollon,
Switzerland, for your warm welcome.

Thank you to the real-life Flavie for sharing your
experiences and your insightful comments.

And thanks to Ajša for your support and friendship.

Marion Brand worked as a shepherdess for a
summer in the Swiss Alps, before deciding to honor
her commitment to nature with pencil and brush.
A graduate in graphic arts and illustration from
HEAD in Geneva, she lives in the Haut-Jura region of
France. *My Life on the Mountain* is her fifth book.